DREAM DOODLE DRAW!
Sweet Treats

By Hannah Eliot

Illustrated by Julie Ingham

LITTLE SIMON

New York London Toronto Sydney New Delhi

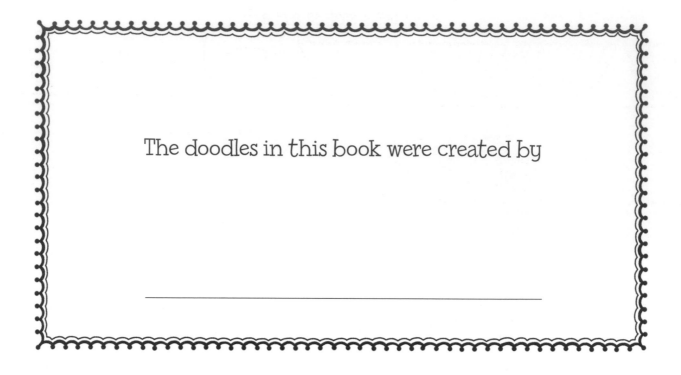

The doodles in this book were created by

_____

LITTLE SIMON

An imprint of Simon & Schuster Children's Publishing Division

1230 Avenue of the Americas, New York, New York 10020

Copyright © 2014 by Simon & Schuster, Inc.

For information about special discounts for bulk purchases, please contact Simon & Schuster Special Sales

at 1-866-506-1949 or business@simonandschuster.com.

The Simon & Schuster Speakers Bureau can bring authors to your live event. For more information or to book an event contact the

Simon & Schuster Speakers Bureau at 1-866-248-3049 or visit our website at www.simonspeakers.com.

Designed by Jay Colvin

Manufactured in China 0214 SCP

First Edition

2 4 6 8 10 9 7 5 3 1

ISBN 978-1-4814-0452-5

Who is ready to bake? Color in this bakery scene,
and let's get started!

Decorate these cupcakes!
What flavor are they? Write the flavors on the lines below.

These doughnuts need some sprinkles!

What's baking inside this oven? Draw it!

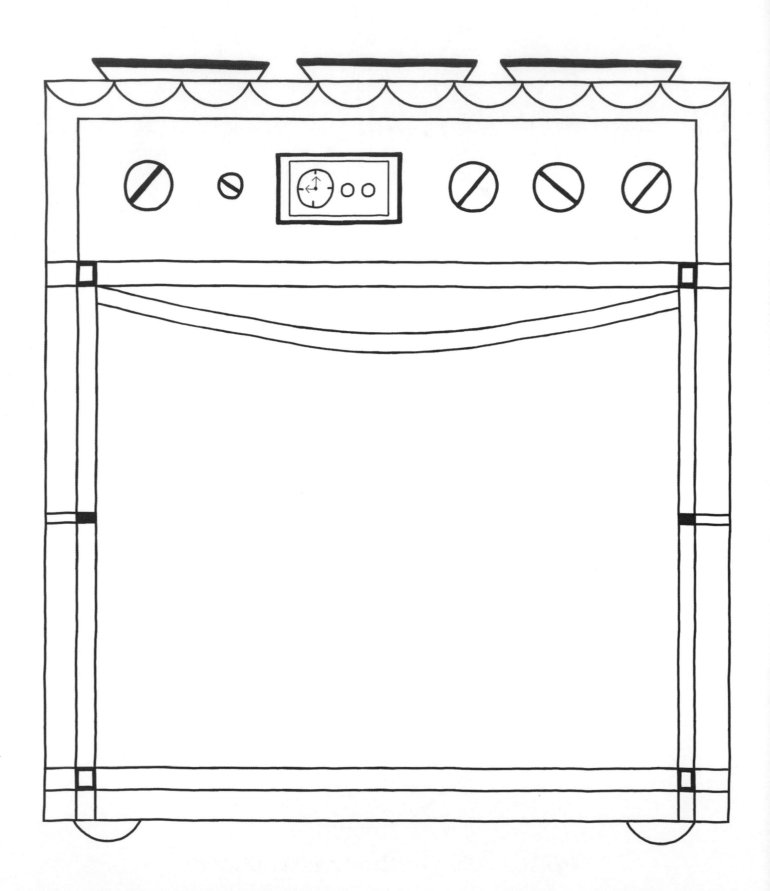

What's cooling on the counter? Draw it!

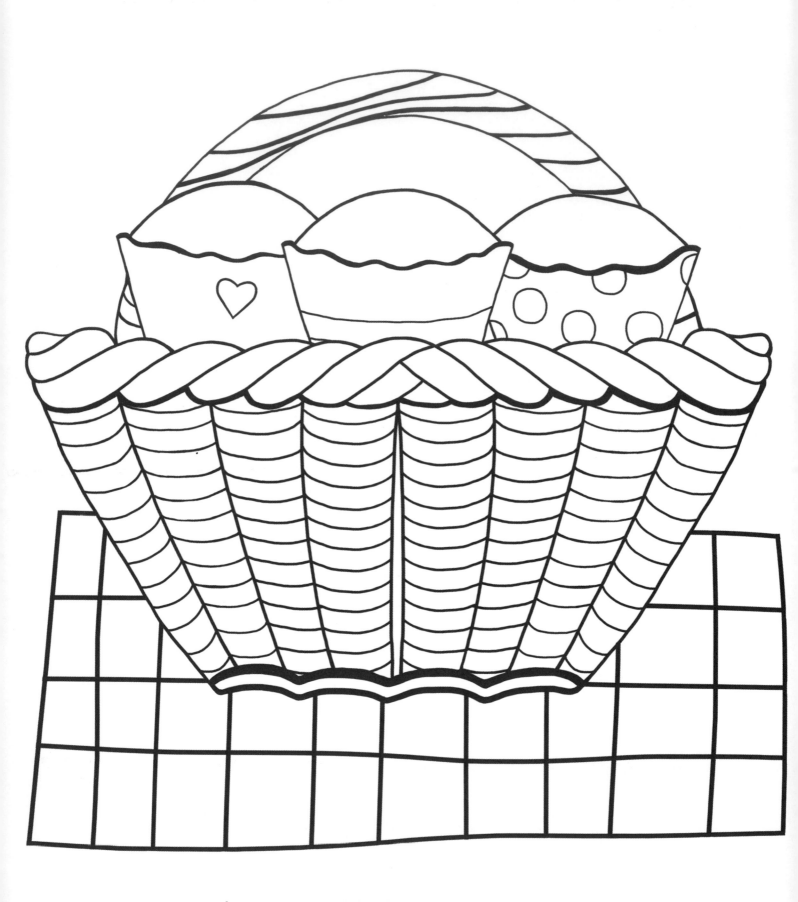

It looks like someone is having a picnic!
What kind of muffins are in the basket?

Draw a delicious treat on the plate next to this glass of milk.

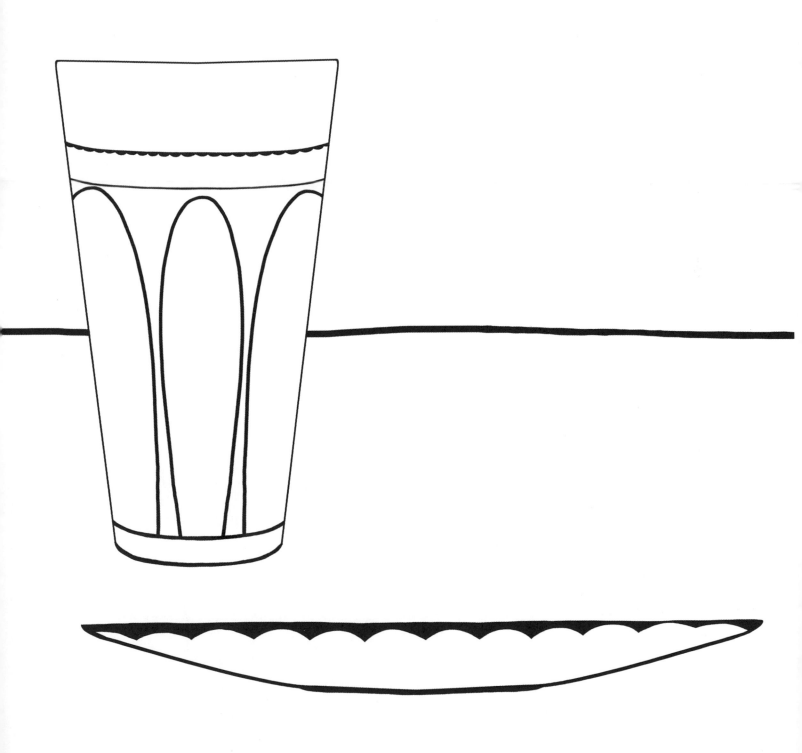

Put your favorite candy toppings on this ice cream!

Put your favorite fruit toppings on *this* ice cream!

Draw polka dots and stripes on the cupcake wrappers.

These cookies need some decoration!

Write something special on this cake.

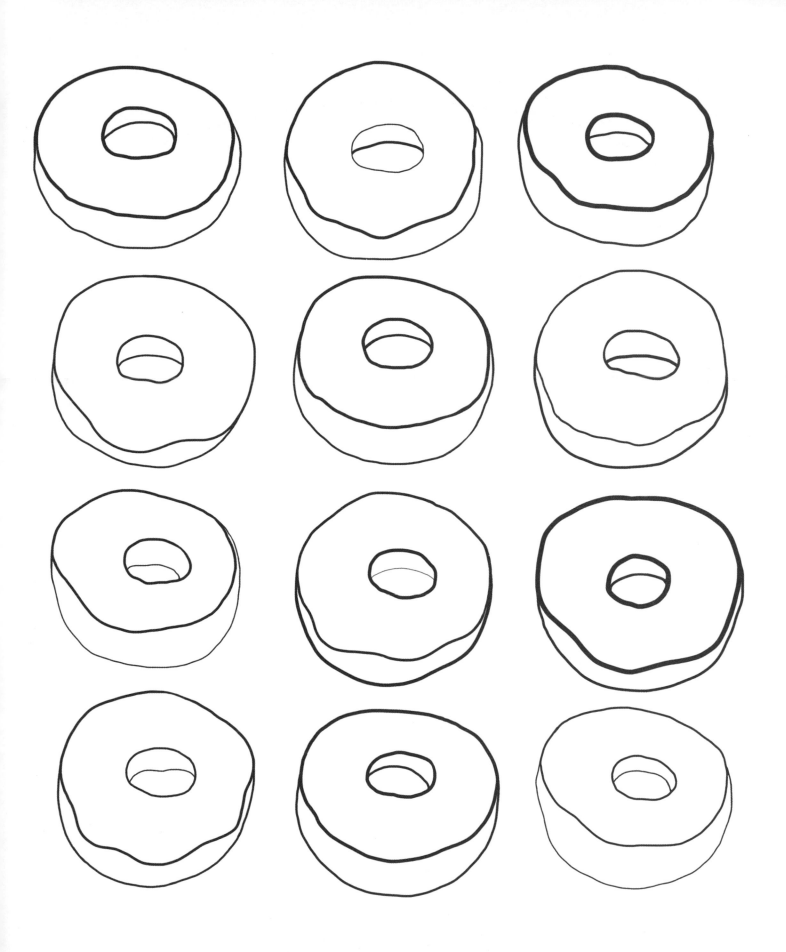

These doughnuts need to be decorated for a party!

Add your favorite treat to this page.

This cake just came out of the oven.

What flavor is each layer? Color the layers!

Whose birthday is it? Decorate the room with streamers and confetti, and add some people if you want!

Now decorate the cake!

Draw smiley faces on these cookies.

Doodle some patterns on these yummy cakes!

These cupcakes need something more—can you
frost and decorate them?

Fill this page with sweet treats!

Connect the dots to see an icy surprise!

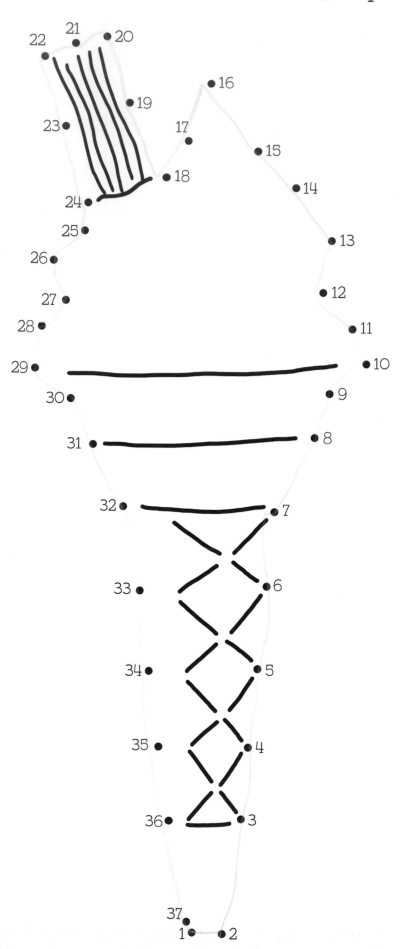

This bakery makes lots of delicious treats!

Looking at the ingredients, can you guess what kind of bread this is?

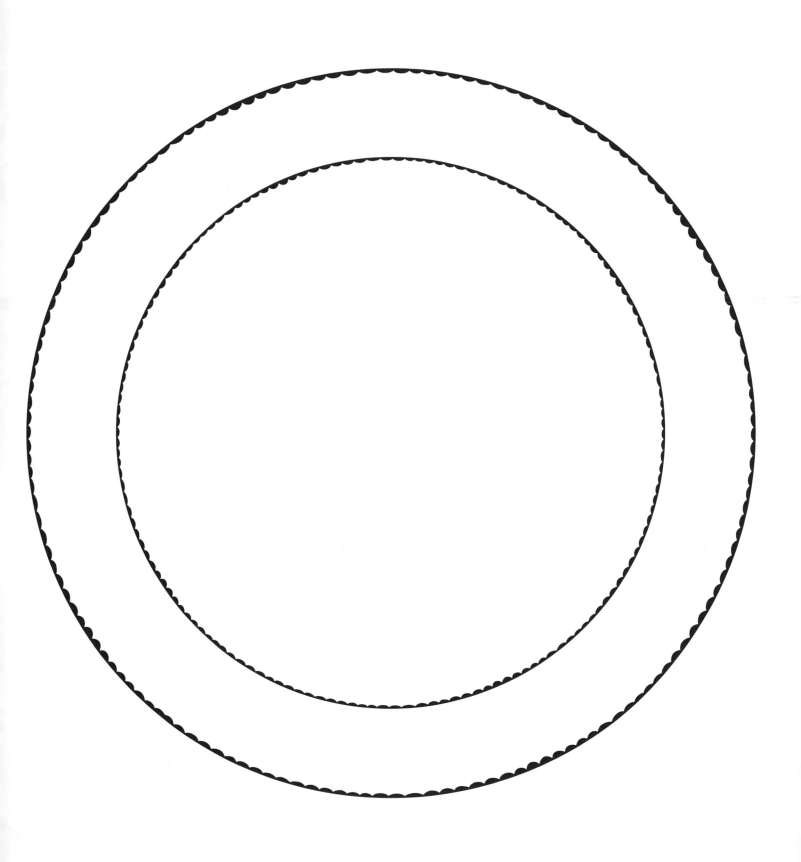

Add your favorite treat to this plate.

These cookies need to get to the oven!

Start

Can you help them find their way?

Finish

Looking at the ingredients, can you guess
what kind of cookies these are?

What's baking inside this oven? Draw it!

What's cooling on the counter? Draw it!

Use the shapes and patterns on this page
to decorate the cake on the next page.

Ice these cookies with your favorite colors.

Color in these sweet treats!

Draw the other half of this cupcake!

Color in these jars of candy.

And add some candy to the bottom jars!

This banana split needs some color!

Color in the cookies and hot chocolate.
Then doodle a cool design on the mug!

Give these doughnuts some sprinkles.

Color in these yummy ice pops!

Connect the dots to see a fruity surprise!

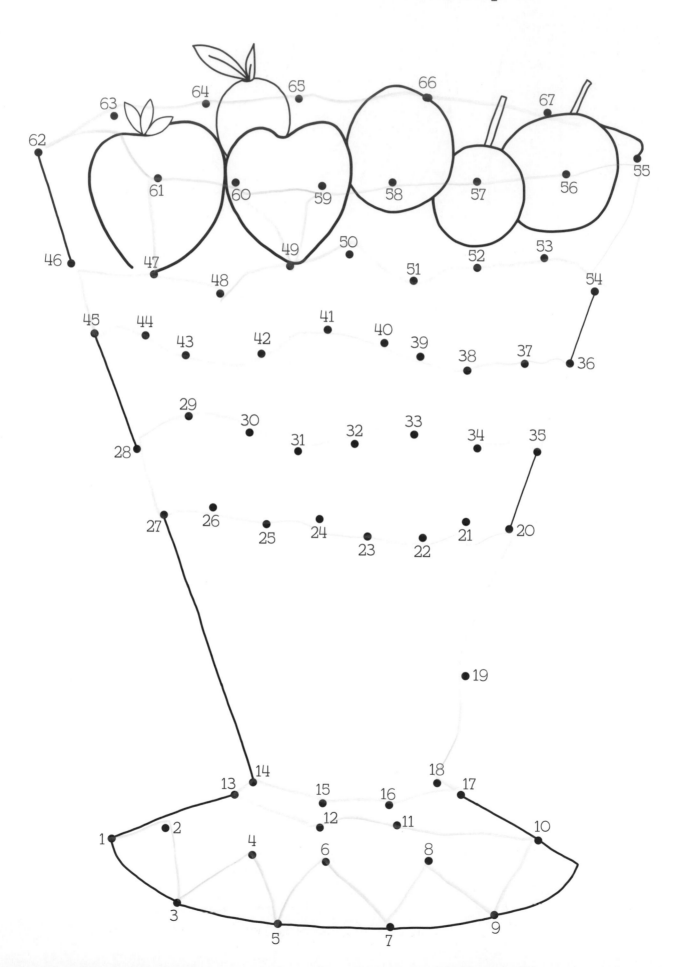

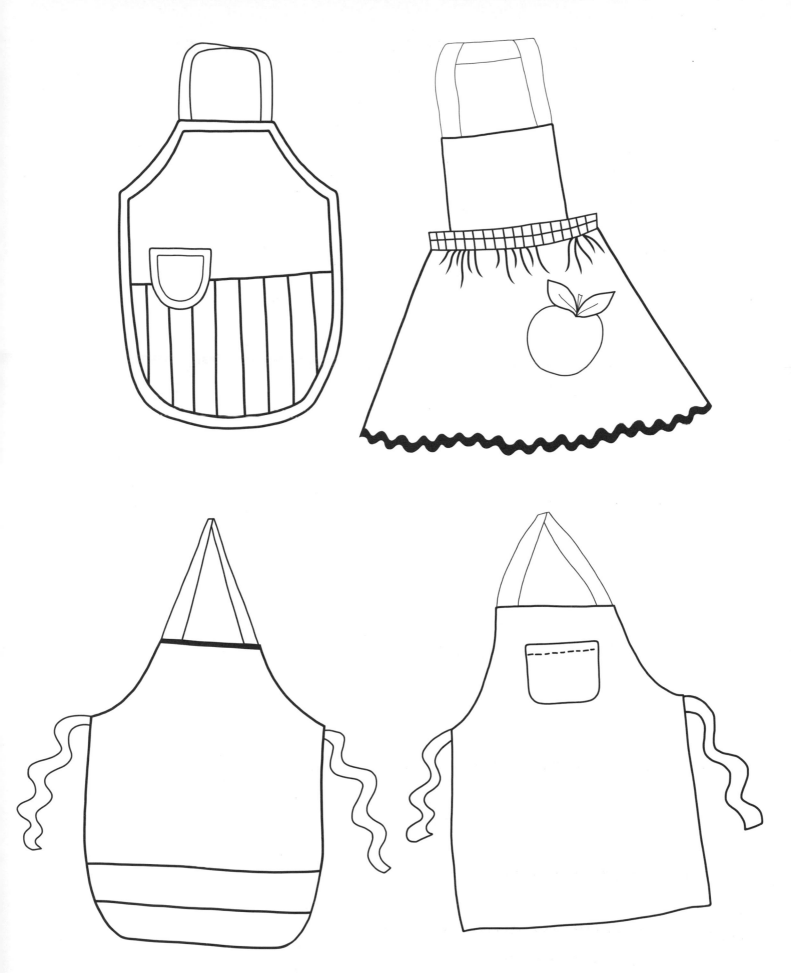

Decorate these aprons.

Draw some more doughnuts on this page!

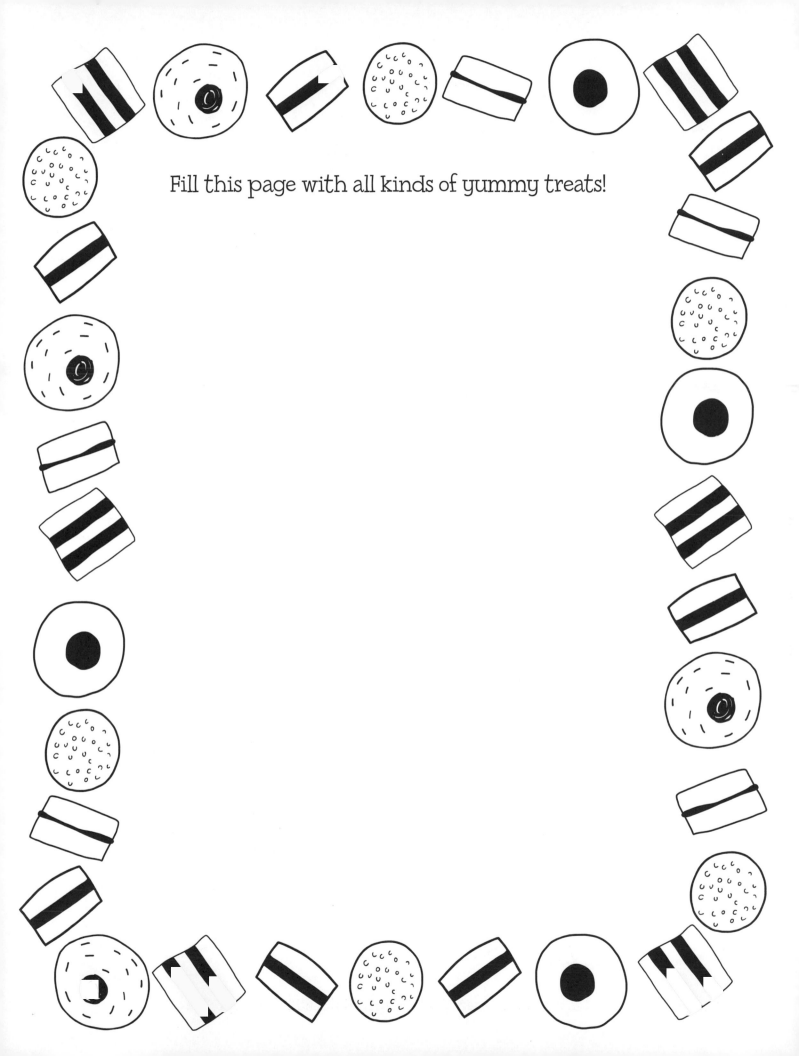

Fill this page with all kinds of yummy treats!

Color in these treats!

These ingredients are for the treat on the next page.
Color them in.

Yum! Now color the fruit tart.

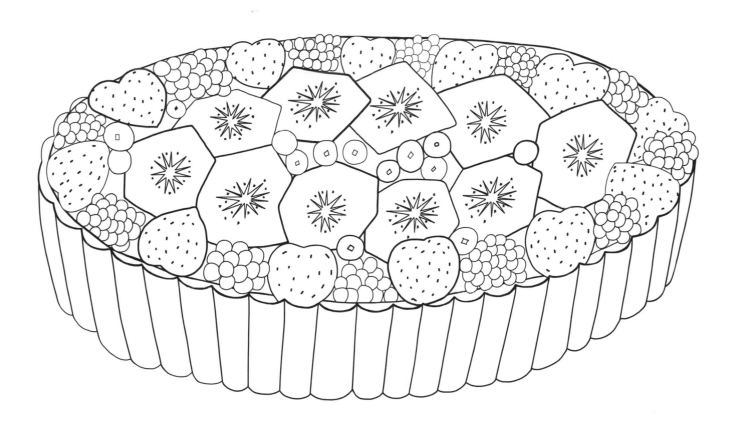

Finish decorating this birthday cake for your best friend!

Color in these lollipops.

Can you spot these images in the scene? Color them in!

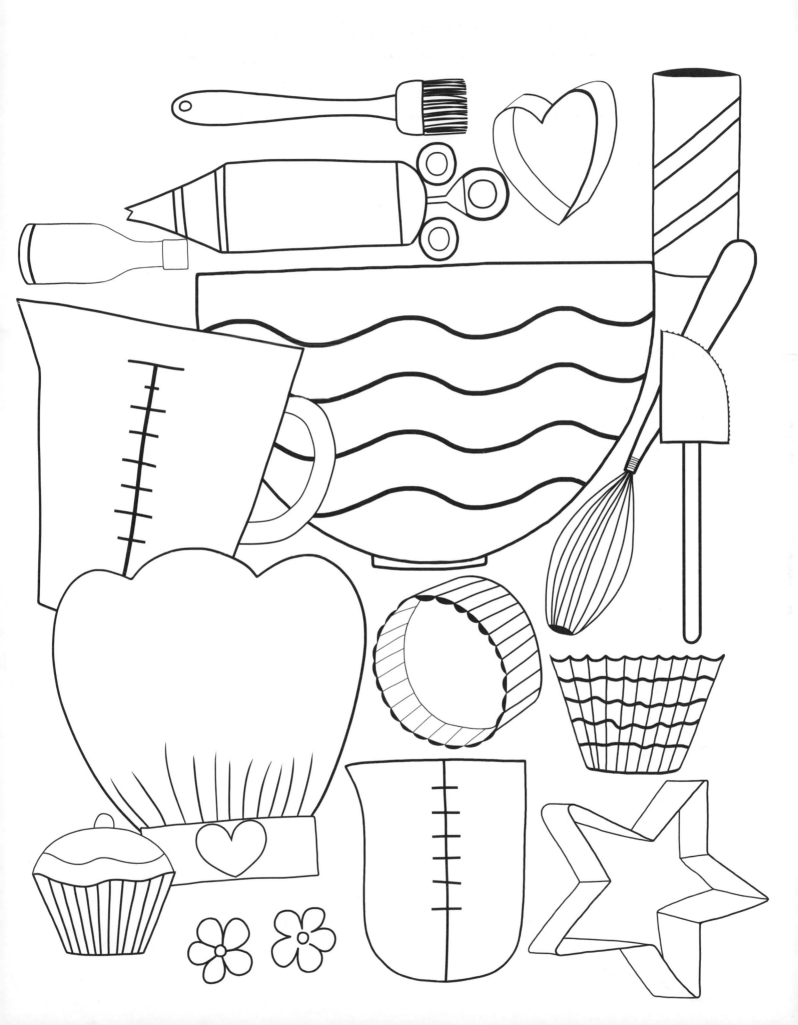

Write something special on the top of this cake.

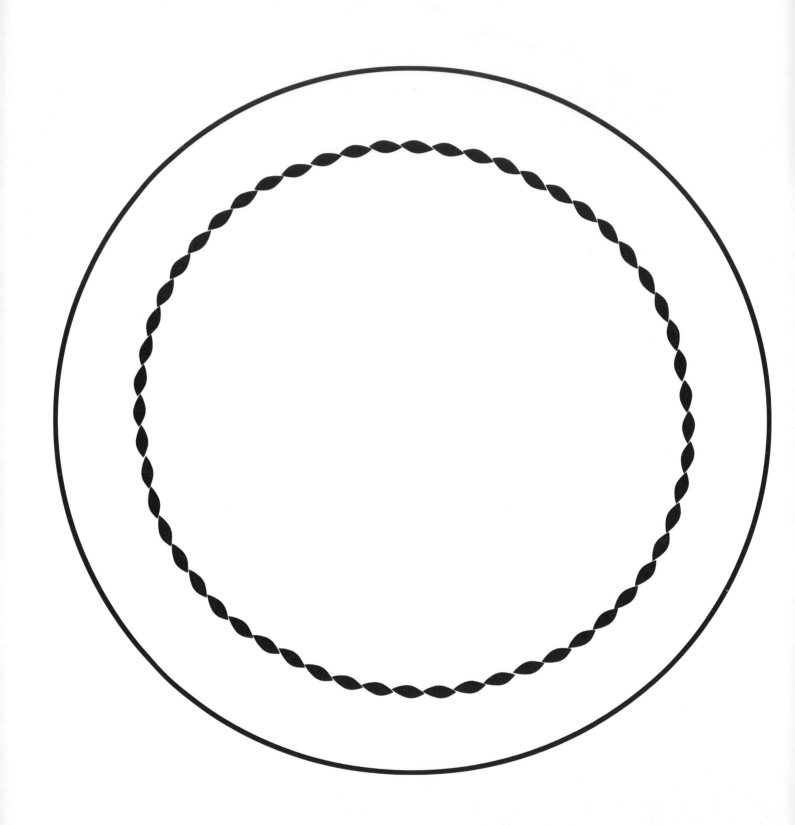

This chef is trying to figure out what to make.
Help him decide by drawing it in his thought bubble!

Hey! Who took bites of those doughnuts?

Draw your own doughnuts!

Can you decorate the cake with the items below?

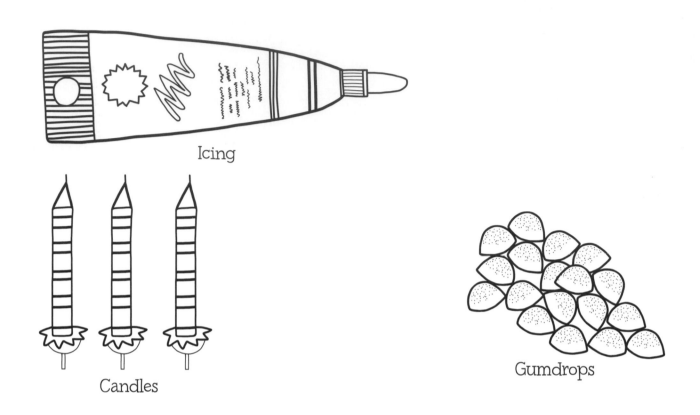

Icing

Candles

Gumdrops

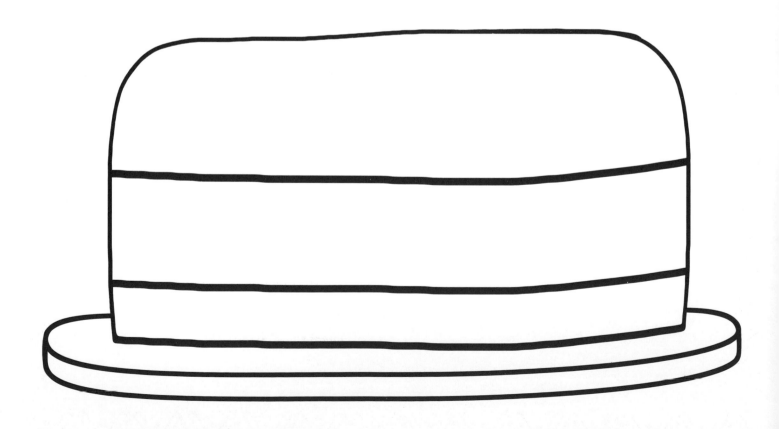

This cake just came out of the oven.
What flavor is each layer? Color the layers!

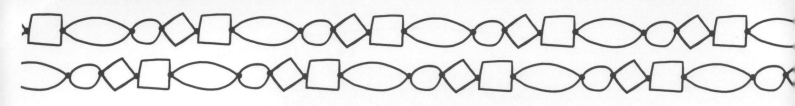

Add your favorite treat to this plate.

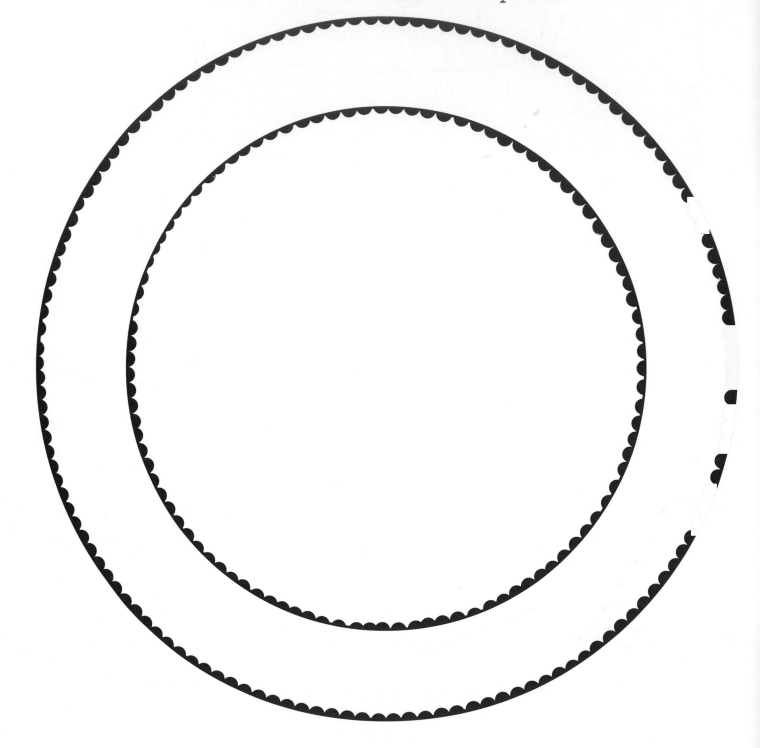

Color in these delicious milkshakes!

These ingredients need to get to the mixing bowl!

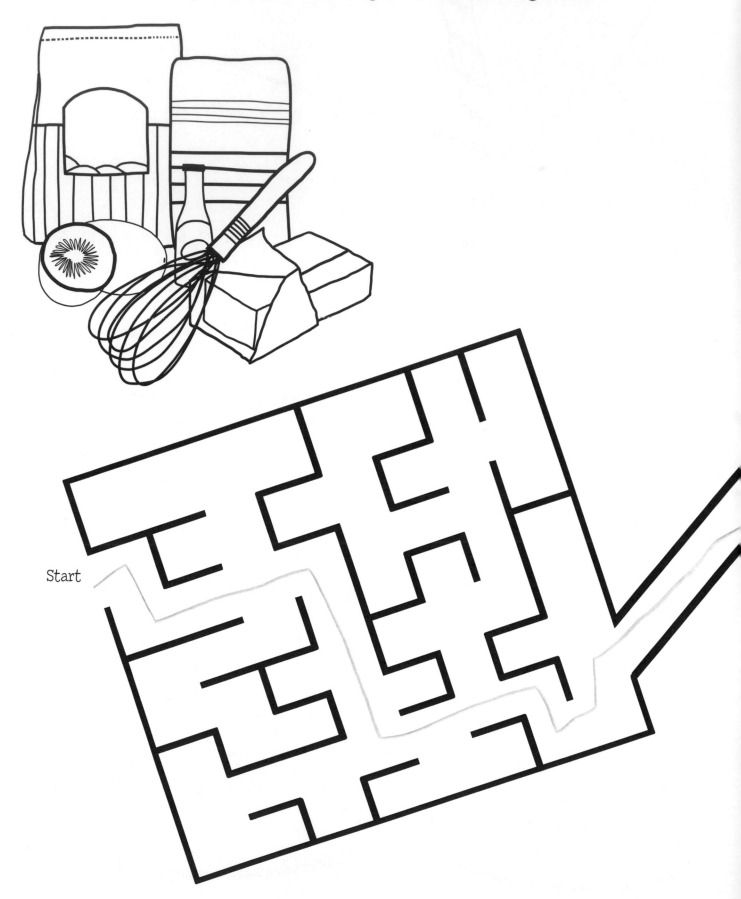

Start

Can you help them find their way?

Finish

Add some ice cream to these cones!

Draw some more candy on this page.

Hey! Whose hand is that in the cookie jar?

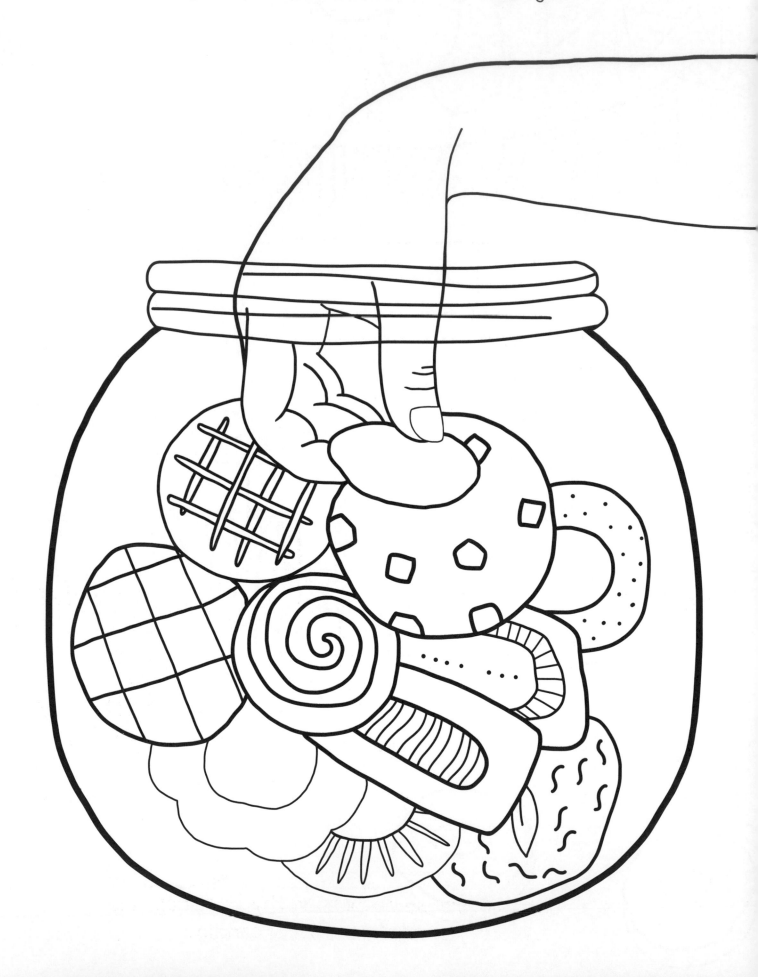

How old are you? Finish decorating this birthday cake
and add the right number of candles.

Looking at the ingredients,
can you guess what kind of muffins are on the next page?

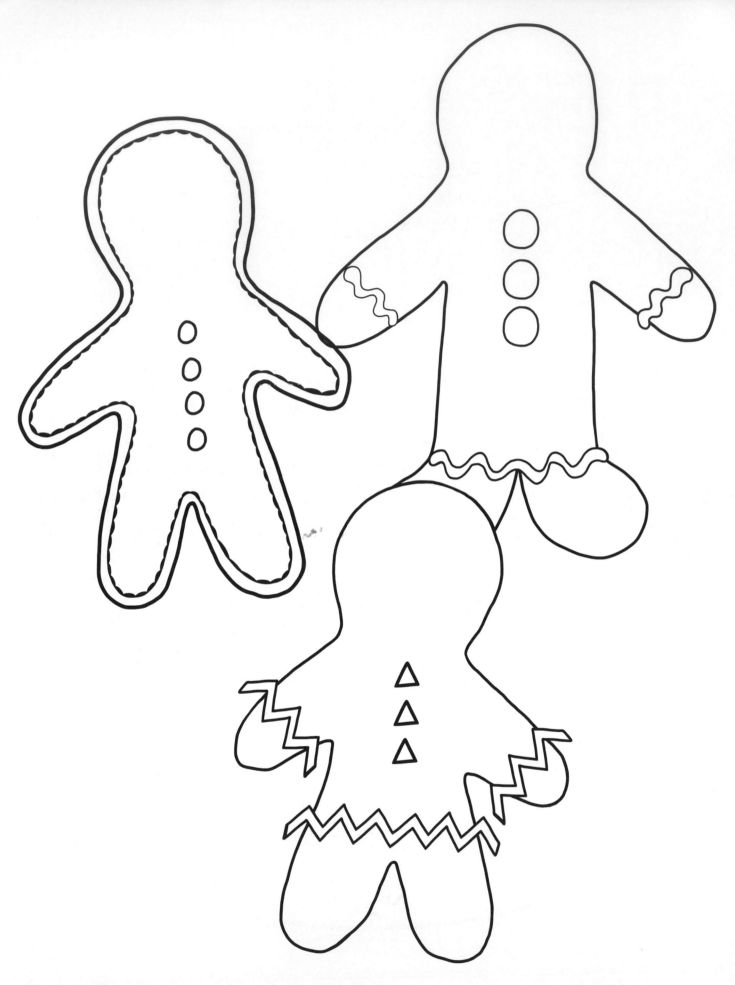

Give these gingerbread cookies some faces and clothes!

Draw the other half of this cake. Then color it in!

Yum! Candy bags!

Color in these pretty pies.

Put your favorite toppings on this ice cream!

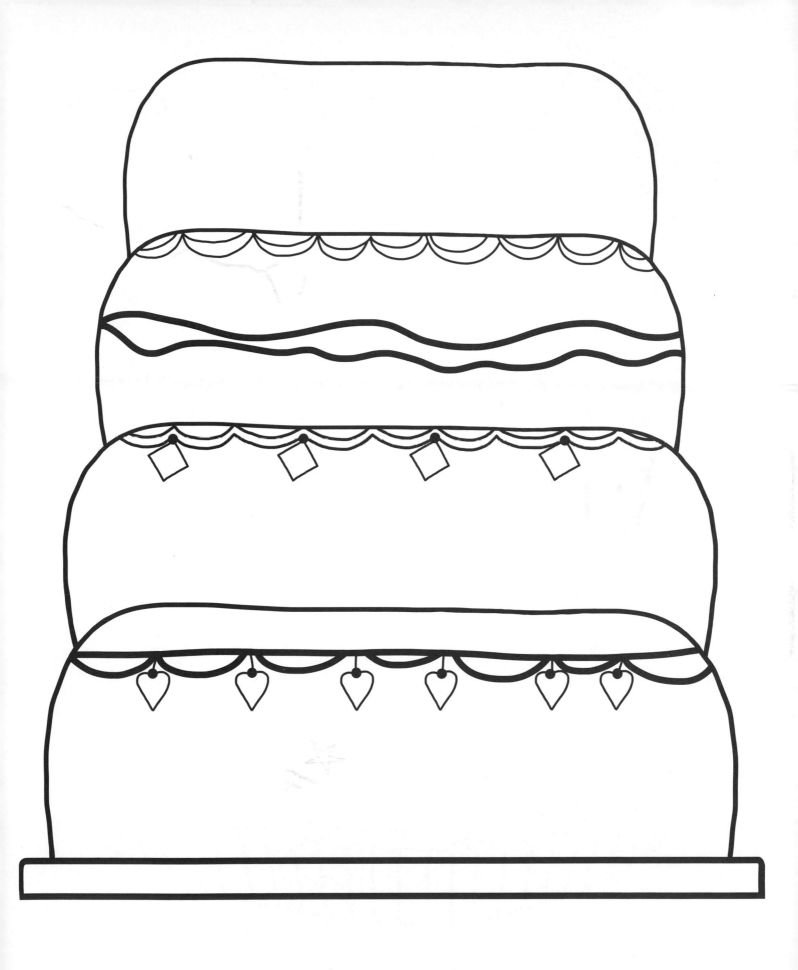

Raspberry

Blueberry

Blackberry

Strawberry

Kiwi

What kind of fruit will go on your fruit tart?

This chef is trying to figure out what to make.
Help her decide by drawing it in her thought bubble!

Connect the dots to see a sweet treat!

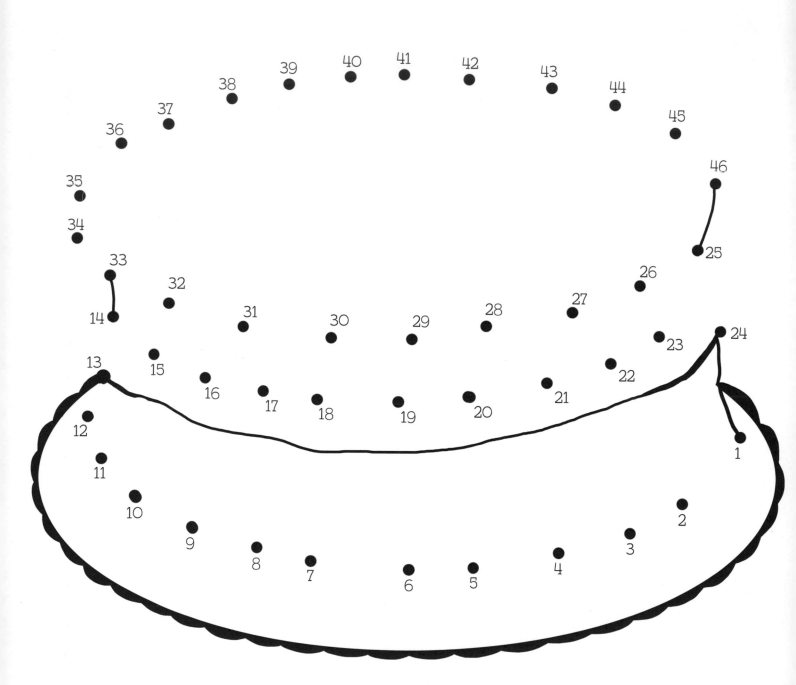

Draw a tasty snack!

Can you spot these images in the scene? Color them in!

Color in these sweet treats!

Decorate these cookies.

These ingredients are for the treat on the next page. Color them in!

Yum! Can you smell the cinnamon rolls?